EARLY BIRD
STORIES

The Dog and the Fox

Early ★ Reader

First American edition published in 2019 by Lerner Publishing Group, Inc.

An original concept by Jenny Jinks
Copyright © 2019 Jenny Jinks

Illustrated by Hanna Wood

First published by Maverick Arts Publishing Limited

Maverick
arts publishing

Licensed Edition
The Dog and the Fox

For the avoidance of doubt, pursuant to Chapter 4 of the Copyright, Designs and Patents Act of 1988, the proprietor asserts the moral right of the Author to be identified as the author of the Work; and asserts the moral right of the Author to be identified as the illustrator of the Work.

Lerner Publications Company
A division of Lerner Publishing Group, Inc.
241 First Avenue North
Minneapolis, MN 55401 USA

For reading levels and more information, look up this title at
www.lernerbooks.com.

Main body text set in Mikado a. Typeface provided by HVD Fonts.

Library of Congress Cataloging-in-Publication Data

Names: Jinks, Jenny, author. | Wood, Hannah, illustrator.
Title: The Dog and the Fox / by Jenny Jinks ; illustrated by Hannah Wood.
Description: First American edition. | Minneapolis : Lerner Publications, 2019. |
    Series: Early bird readers. Yellow (Early bird stories).
Identifiers: LCCN 2018018411 (print) | LCCN 2018025410 (ebook) |
    ISBN 9781541543331 (eb pdf) | ISBN 9781541541719 (lb : alk. paper) |
    ISBN 9781541546301 (pb : alk. paper)
Subjects: LCSH: Readers—Animals. | Readers (Primary) | Animals—Juvenile
    literature.
Classification: LCC PE1127.A6 (ebook) | LCC PE1127.A6 J56 2019 (print) |
    DDC 428.6/2—dc23

LC record available at https://lccn.loc.gov/2018018411

Manufactured in the United States of America
1-45345-38995-6/26/2018

EARLY BIRD STORIES

The Dog and the Fox

Jenny Jinks

Illustrated by
Hannah Wood

Lerner Publications ◆ Minneapolis

The sun is up and so is Dog.

Dog is bored. He wants to play.

Dog gets a ball and runs to Fox.

"Get up," says Dog.

But Fox does not.

Dog digs up a bone.

It is big.

"Get up," says Dog.

But Fox does not.

Dog runs in the sun.

He gets hot.

"Get up," says Dog.

But Fox does not.

Dog jumps in the pond.

He is wet.

"Get up," says Dog.

But Fox does not.

Dog sits in the sun.

He is worn out.

"Get up," says Dog.

But Fox does not.

The moon is up and so is Fox.

Fox is bored.

He wants to play.

Fox gets a ball and runs to Dog.

"Get up," says Fox.

But Dog does not.

Quiz

1. The sun is up and . . . ?
   a) So is Fox
   b) So is Frog
   c) So is Dog

2. What does Dog take to Fox?
   a) A ball and a bone
   b) A boot
   c) A cake

3. Why does Dog get hot?
   a) He jumps in a pond.
   b) He runs in the sun.
   c) He walks with Fox.

4. Where does Dog jump?
   a) In the mud
   b) Into bed
   c) In the pond

5. What is Dog doing when Fox wants
   to play?
   a) Sleeping
   b) Running
   c) Digging

Leveled for Guided Reading

Early Bird Stories have been edited and leveled by leading educational consultants to correspond with guided reading levels. The levels are assigned by taking into account the content, language style, layout, and phonics used in each book.

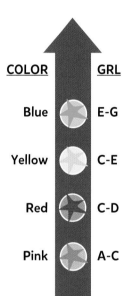

COLOR	GRL
Blue	E-G
Yellow	C-E
Red	C-D
Pink	A-C